Barry Loser
hates half term!

Absolutely nothing to do with

Jim Smith

Pirate camp

It was the first Sunday of half term and I was sitting in my sitting room watching **Future Ratboy** with my best friends, Bunky and Nancy Verkenwerken.

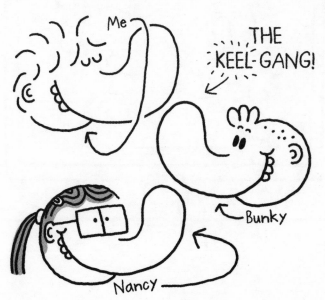

Me

,,,,,THE
KEEL-GANG!

Bunky

Nancy

5

'This is gonna be the keelest half term EVER!' I said.

'Keel' is how **Future Ratboy**, my favourite TV superhero, says 'cool', in case you didn't know.

Future Ratboy

Not Bird

6

'YEAH!' said Bunky, who's sort of like **Future Ratboy**'s sidekick, Not Bird, except he's not a bird. 'I'm SO glad we don't have to go to babyish old Pirate Camp any more!'

'Me too!' I said. 'Pirate Camp is for BABIES!'

slightly over-excited

Pirate Camp is the holiday camp that me, Bunky and Nancy used to go to every half term when we were younger. It's sort of like a nursery for kiddywinkles, except it's on Mogden Island, which is an island in the middle of Mogden Lake.

It's owned by an unbelievakeely old man called Burt Barnacle, who dresses up as a pirate and goes on about treasure the whole time.

He says there's a whole chest of it,
buried somewhere on the island.
Not that we ever found any when
we were there.

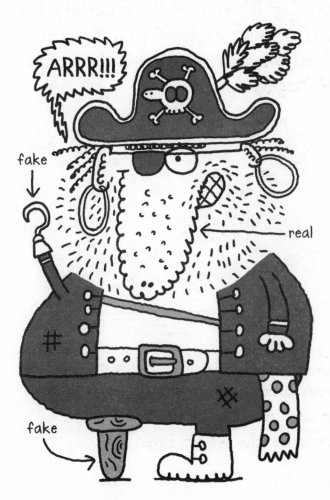

'I mean, who wants to sit around a campfire singing songs about trees for a whole week?' said Bunky, waggling his hands in the air, which is how he does his impression of a tree.

a tree

Bunky

'YE-AH! Singing songs about trees is for KIDDYWINKLES!' I said, remembering sitting round the campfire at Pirate Camp with Bunky and Nancy, singing about trees.

Sitting round a campfire singing about trees wasn't the only thing we did at Pirate Camp, by the way. There was also pirate face-painting, pirate raft-making, lying under Burt's giant skull-and-crossbones parachute while he whooshed it up and down, and listening to him tell super-spookoid ghost stories before we went to sleep in our tents at night.

all those things I just said

I was just realising that I actukeely quite liked some of the stuff we got up to at Pirate Camp when my mum walked into the room carrying a plateful of Feeko's chocolate digestive biscuits and three cans of Fronkle.

'Here you go, kiddywinkles!' she said, ruffling my hair.

looks a bit like Burt's nose, except upside down

'MU-UM! We're not KIDDYWINKLES any more!' I said, sliding a biscuit off the plate and slotting it into my mouth.

my mouth slot

SLOT!

me slotting

'Apologies for my mother,' I said to Bunky and Nancy, and they both sniggled.

'MAUREEN?' cried my dad from upstairs. 'MAUREEN, DESMOND'S POOED HIS NAPPY AGAIN!'

boring drawing alert

My dad was talking about my baby brother, Desmond Loser the Second, in case you didn't know.

poo stink

'WELL, CHANGE IT THEN!' screamed
my mum up the stairs, and she turned
back to us and started ringing. Which
was weird, because she isn't a phone.
She's my mum.

a phone

my mum

Great Aunt Mildred

'My new phone!' smiled my mum, pulling a huge great big shiny white phone out of her pocket and sliding her finger across the screen. 'Loser residence!' she said, holding it up to her ear.

'What's that I'm looking at?' crackled a voice out of the phone's speaker. 'Is that an ear or something?'

'Ooh, must be a video call!' said my mum all proudly, and she took the phone away from her ear and looked at the screen. 'Aunt Mildred!' she smiled.

one second

the next second

I hopped off the sofa and ran over to my mum, tiptoeing a centimetre higher so I could see the screen too. 'Hi, Great Aunt Mildred!' I said, spluttering biscuit crumbs all over Great Aunt Mildred's face, which was staring back at me.

exackerly like Burt's nose

It was at about this moment in the history of the universe that I noticed that Great Aunt Mildred's nose was about three times its usual size.

'Are you OK, Aunt Mildred?' said my mum. 'Your nose looks a bit . . . puffy.'

'That's why I'm calling,' said Great Aunt Mildred. 'This little blighter bit me on the end of my hooter just now and the whole thing's swollen up like an air bag!'

She held a jam jar up to the screen. Inside was a bright green beetle with six red legs and a humungaloid pair of pincers. 'I was reaching for a banana when it jumped out of the fruit bowl!' she warbled.

little blighter

Bunky and Nancy slid off their bits of the sofa and ran over to have a look at Great Aunt Mildred's nose. 'She's right - it DOES look like an air bag!' chuckled Bunky, as Nancy peered into the jam jar on the screen.

'Where are your bananas from?' asked Nancy.

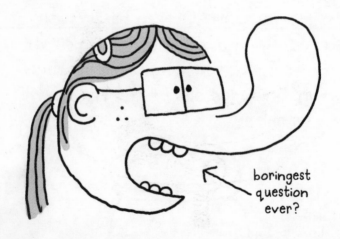

boringest question ever?

'Feeko's Supermarket, of course!' said Great Aunt Mildred.

'No, I meant what country!' said Nancy, and Great Aunt Mildred put the jam jar down and wandered off, then reappeared a millisecond later holding a banana.

'Sticker says "Grown in Smeldovia",' said Great Aunt Mildred, and Nancy gasped.

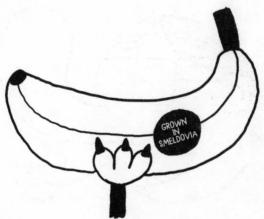

'I knew I recognised that insect - it's a Smeldovian Biting Banana Beetle,' Nancy said. 'They're extremely poisonous!'

I looked at Bunky and raised my
favourite eyebrow.

super
keel

hate
this
one

'Typikeel Nancy!' I said, seeing as she
always knows stuff like that -
especially since she'd started going
along to her dad's loserish nature club.

'POISONOUS?' gasped Great Aunt
Mildred, grabbing her nose. 'What
does that mean?' she whimpered.

'It means I'm coming round right now!'
said my mum.

Party time

'Call you when I get there!' cried my mum, reversing out of the driveway, and we all waved. She'd thrown her travel bag into the back seat of her car, seeing as Great Aunt Mildred lived about eight million miles away and she'd have to stay until she was better, which might be all week.

'B-but, Maureen . . .' warbled my dad,
bending over to pick up Desmond Loser
the Second. 'What about my bad back?
I can't look after Barry and Desmond
all on my own!'

bad

'Oh don't be pathetic, Kenneth!' said my
mum, honking the horn, and she was
gone. Which meant . . .

24

'PARTY TIME!' I shouted, running back into the sitting room. I forward-rolled on to the sofa and flopped my legs over the back of it, settling down to watch the rest of **Future Ratboy**, upside-down-stylee. 'This half term is gonna be AMAZEKEEL!'

'It is NOT party time!' shouted my dad, marching into the room and plonking Desmond on the carpet. 'ARGH, MY BACK!' he cried, taking about three hours to straighten up again.

Future Ratboy ended and I flipped
myself backwards off the sofa,
somersaulting through the air and
landing bum-first on the coffee table.
'I know - let's jump up and down on
my mum and dad's bed!' I cried,
waggling my hands around like a tree.

'Keelness times a millikeels!' shouted
Bunky, and me, him and Nancy all
ran upstairs.

The stink

'THAT'S ENOUGH!' boomed my dad, barging into the bedroom once we'd been bouncing up and down on the bed long enough for his bedside table to have juddered halfway across the room. He plonked Desmond down and something went snap. 'MY BACK!' he screamed again, waddling over to the bed and flomping down on it, bent in half like an L.

'POOWEE, what's that stink?' snuffled Bunky, jumping off the bed and waggling his nose in the air, and we all looked at Desmond.

Desmond's face had turned red and his eyes were rolling in their sockets.

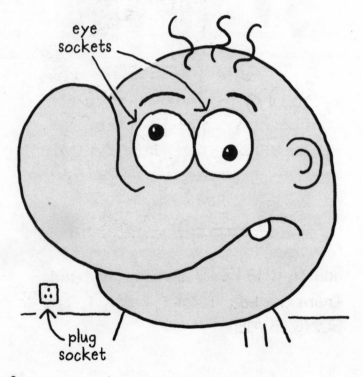

eye sockets

plug socket

'Er, Da-ad? I think Desmond's doing another poo-oo?' I said, sniggling to Bunky and Nancy, and they both bent in half like Ls too, except out of laughter instead of pain.

for ← Loser!

'RIGHT, THAT'S IT!' shouted my dad from the bed. 'BUNKY, NANCY, YOU'RE GOING HOME!'

Wiping someone else's bum

'Apologies for my father – I'll call you later,' I said, as Bunky and Nancy walked off down the road, and I slammed the front door and stomped back upstairs to my mum and dad's room. 'THANK YOU VERY MUCH INDEED!' I shouted, once I got there.

My dad was lying on the floor, wiping Desmond's bum. 'I can't do this, Barry...' he whimpered, still bent in half like an L.

more like an O, actukeely

'You look like you're doing fine to me,' I said, thinking how there was no way I was EVER going to have a baby, seeing as it's bad enough wiping my OWN bum, let alone someone else's too.

31

'That's not what I meant,' said my dad, passing me a plastic bag full of poo.

'What DID you mean, then?' I said, except it came out as 'Dot DID do deen, den?' because I'd stuffed two of my spare fingers up my nostrils.

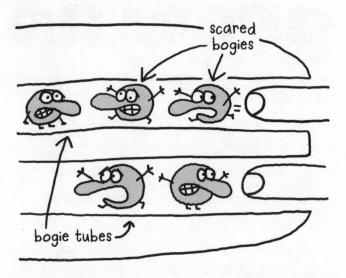

scared bogies

bogie tubes

'I can't look after you and Desmond on my own, Barry,' said my dad. 'I think you might have to go to Pirate Camp for the rest of half term . . .'

Time to grow up

'But I don't WANT to go to Pirate Camp!' I shouted for the millikeelth time, thirteen and three quarter hours later. It was Monday morning and I was sitting in the back seat of my dad's car on the way to Mogden Pier, which is where the ferry for Mogden Island leaves from.

'Why not?' said my dad. 'I thought you LOVED Pirate Camp.'

'I USED to love Pirate Camp, but not any more . . . it's for BABIES!' I cried, and Desmond, who was sitting next to me in his baby seat, started giggling.

VROOM!

'You should fit in there just perfectly, then!' said my dad, and I screwed my face up and stared at him in the rear-view mirror.

'What in the unkeelness does THAT mean?' I whined.

'You're a big brother now, Barry,' said my dad. 'You can't go screaming round the house acting like a kiddywinkle any more . . .'

'I am NOT a KIDDYWINKLE!' I shouted, stomping my feet on the car's carpet and crossing my arms.

me when I was a kiddywinkle

'Yes, well, until you can prove you've grown up a bit, I'm afraid you'll need to stay on Mogden Island with all the other little babies,' said my dad.

actukeely not this small

'I bet MUM wouldn't send me to Pirate Camp!' I shouted.

'As a matter of fact, I spoke to your mum on the phone this morning and she thinks it's a great idea,' said my dad. 'Who knows - maybe you'll surprise yourself and enjoy it!'

'Maybe you'll surprise YOURself!' I shouted, which didn't really make sense, but I wasn't in the mood to care. 'Thanks for ruining my half term!' I grumbled, and I stared out of the window at the ginormous billboard we were driving past.

billboard
(leaving it blank
so I don't spoil
next page)

Donald Cox

'ANOTHER FANTASTIC DONALD COX DEVELOPMENT!' boomed the words on the billboard, next to a mahoosive photo of a man in a suit with sunglasses on. That makes it sound like the suit was wearing sunglasses - it wasn't, the man was.

The man with the sunglasses on was Donald Cox, who's been building buildings all over Mogden recently. In the photo he was standing in front of some skyscrapers, with his hands spread out like he was the king of Mogden.

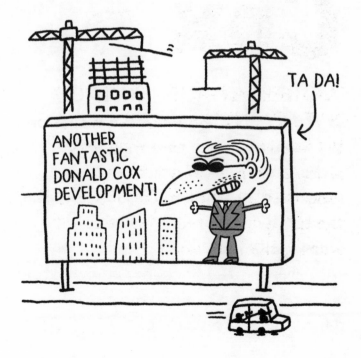

Behind the billboard, half a real-life skyscraper was sticking out of the ground. Men in yellow plastic hats were dotted around all over it, hammering planks and eating sandwiches.

scariest lunch ever

'Blooming Donald Cox,' grumbled my dad, pressing the back-massage button on the side of his seat, and the whole thing started to vibrate.

40

'You can't go five metres without seeing his face these days,' he said, and he turned left down Bunky's road, which everyone knows is the shortest short cut to Mogden Pier.

I pressed my nose up against the car window and spotted Bunky standing outside his house talking to Nancy and her dad, Mr Verkenwerken. Which didn't surprise me, seeing as they're next-door neighbours.

'DONALD COX!' I boomed, waving at Bunky. I've started calling Bunky 'Donald Cox' sometimes, by the way, because it makes him wee his pants with laughter.

Bunky
Cox

Bunky carried on standing there, chatting to Nancy and Mr Verkenwerken and not weeing his pants at all, and I realised I hadn't wound my window down.

I wound my window down and took a deep breath. 'DONALD COX!' I boomed again, and Bunky and Nancy jumped.

'DONALD COX!' boomed Bunky back, because he's started calling me 'Donald Cox' too.

'Help me, Donald - my dad's kidnapped me!' I shouted, imagining I was **Future Ratboy**, and I'd been captured by his number one enemy, Mr X, and locked up in the back of Mr X's giant metal scorpion.

HA! HA HA HA

Mr X

'He's sending me to Pirate Camp, Donald!' I screamed, pounding my fists against the air, miming like I hadn't wound the window down at all. 'Meet me at Mogden Pier!' I wailed, and I wound the window up again and went back to comperleeterly unenjoying my half term.

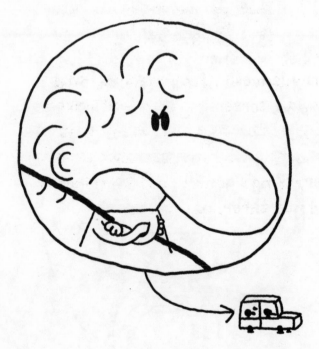

Mogden Pier

'Ferry leaves in four minutes,' said
my dad, screeching to a halt next to
Mogden Pier, and I sat in my seat
wondering why my dad always says
everything's gonna be FOUR minutes,
and not three, or five.

'Maybe it's because he's got FOUR fingers,' I mumbled to myself, as my dad undid his seatbelt. 'Maybe if he had seventeen fingers, everything would take SEVENTEEN minutes instead!'

I think I was just trying to put off getting out of the car.

my dad's new hand

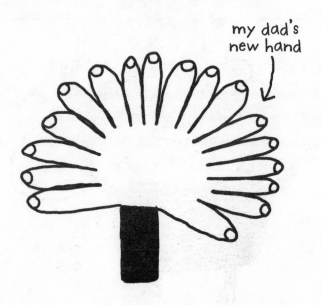

My dad walked round to Desmond's door and lifted him out, careful not to make his back go snap again. 'Come on, Barry, out you pop too,' he chirped, trying not to sound like a horrible dad who was sending his number one son off to a prison camp on an island in the middle of a lake with none of his friends for the whole of half term.

evil
dad

I slid myself out of the car and collapsed in a heap of Barryness on the tarmac.

'Pleeease don't make me go to Pirate Camp!' I cried, as a little girl from about three million years below me at school walked past with her mum on the way to the ferry, giggling at my loserosity.

heap of
Barryness

'Sorry, Barry,' said my dad, holding Desmond's bum up to his nostrils, checking if he'd done another poo. 'Maybe when your Great Aunt Mildred's nose shrinks back to normal and your mum comes home we can have another think.'

The tarmac rumbled and Bunky and Nancy skidded their bikes to a stop and jumped off, panting from cycling all the way to Mogden Pier in less time than it takes to say this sentence.

=WHOOSH!

'What in the name of unkeelness is going on here?' said Bunky, and I explained to him and Nancy how my dad was sending me to Pirate Camp because we'd been jumping up and down on my mum and dad's bed the day before.

happy then

'. . . so really it's kind of you two's fault as well,' I said, getting up from the tarmac and heaving my rucksack out of the boot. My orange tent was strapped to the bottom, with the word 'LOSER' written on it in big black capitals.

'But Pirate Camp is for kiddywinkles!' said Bunky, and my dad was just about to open his mouth and say his thing about how that meant I'd fit in there just perfectly, when I spotted the tip of Darren Darrenofski's nose.

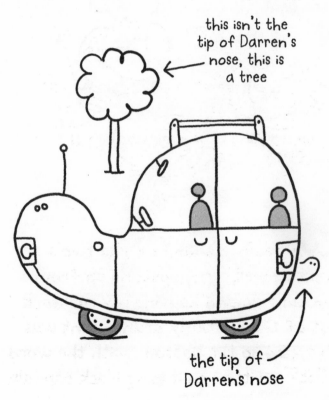

this isn't the tip of Darren's nose, this is a tree

the tip of Darren's nose

Clowny Wowny

'Off to Baby Camp, eh, Loser?' said Darren from my class at school, his mean little piggy face appearing from behind a Darren-Darrenofski's-head-shaped car. He was wearing earphones and carrying a can of root beer flavour Fronkle.

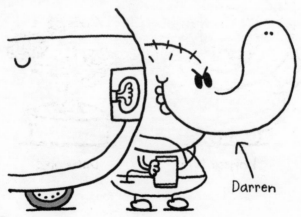

Darren

'BUUURRRPPP!!!' he burped, and an invisible little cloud of stink floated out of his mouth, towards my baby brother's nostrils.

'WAHHH!!!' screamed Desmond, waggling his little hands in the air like a bonsai tree.

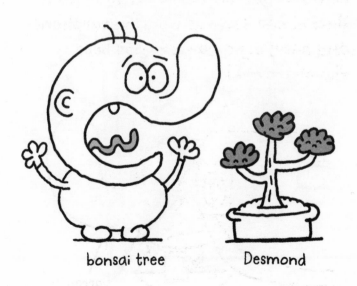

bonsai tree   Desmond

My dad passed Desmond over to Nancy and whipped a scratched-up pink plastic rectangle out of his pocket. 'Here's your mum's old phone, Barry - in case you need to get in touch. I don't want you using up all the battery watching your Future Ratman episodes though,' he said.

flower sticker on back

'Ooh, nice pink phone, Mrs Loser!' snortled Darren, rummaging around in HIS pocket and pulling out a crumpled-up rectangle of card, pretending he was a businessman like Donald Cox or something. 'Here's my number - let's do lunch sometime.'

Darren Darrenofski
number one fan of
Fronkle in the wor
555 8424

I looked down at the smelly bit of paper. 'Darren Darrenofski - number one fan of Fronkle in the world,' it said. Underneath the writing was a Darrenish-looking phone number.

I Future-Ratboy-speed-dialled the number and Darren's pocket started to ring. 'Darrenofski residence,' he said, clicking a button halfway up his earphone wire.

'Er... what in the unkeelness are you doing here, Dazzoid?' I said into my phone.

Darren took a slurp on his Fronkle and burped again. 'Oh nothing, I was just passing . . .' he said, looking a teeny weeny bit shifty-wifty, and I wondered if he'd been wandering around Mogden all on his own, hoping to bump into someone to play it keel with.

really
lonely

You know how Desmond had been screaming from Darren's burp going up his nostrils? Well that was still happening.

'Don't cry, Dezzy,' said Nancy, reaching into Desmond's car seat and pulling out his cuddly toy clown.

Clowny Wowny

Desmond stopped screaming and reached out for his clown. 'Cwowny!' he gurgled, trying to say its name, which is 'Clowny Wowny', the loserest name ever.

'Hewwo, my name is Clowny Wowny!' said Nancy to Desmond, doing her Clowny Wowny impression, and I rolled the two eyeball-shaped gobstoppers in my pocket, which I'd brought along to keep me company on Mogden Island.

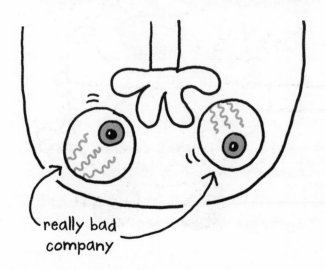

really bad company

Clowny Wowny is the loserish clown character that all the kiddywinkles watch on TV these days. All that happens in a whole episode is that Clowny Wowny wobbles around in his stupid giant clown shoes, falling over stuff and doing blowoffs.

PARP!

'I can't believe the rubbish they put on TV these days, Donald,' I said to Bunky.

'I know, Donald, it's not like when we were kids,' Bunky said, doing a back-to-front-reverse-upside-down-salute, which is what **Future Ratboy** does when he's agreeing with someone.

I looked at my two best friends and waggled my favourite eyebrow, and my least favourite one too. 'Come with me, PLEEEASE?' I whimpered, missing them both already, even though they were standing in front of my eyebrows.

'I'm sorry, Barry, we're just too old for Pirate Camp . . .' said Nancy, peering down at the floor.

bit of gravel

'Plus we're going on a Poo Tour with Nancy's dad today!' said Bunky. 'We were just about to come round yours and tell you when you drove past!'

I rewound my brain to them standing outside their houses, talking to Mr Verkenwerken. 'A Poo Tour?' I cried. 'What in the unkeelness is that?'

what Mr Verkenwerken looks like

'It's where Mr Verkenwerken walks us round the countryside, pointing out all the different animals' poos!' sniggled Bunky, as Nancy took her glasses off.

guess the poo!

'It's more of a NATURE tour really,' she said, cleaning them on her skirt. 'My dad just calls it a Poo Tour to get people like you and Bunky interested. We mostly walk around looking at flowers and insects and stuff . . .'

'AND POO!' shouted Bunky, and I fast-forwarded my brain to how keel the Poo Tour was going to be. Not that I was going to be on it.

Darren put his hand on my shoulder and took another slurp of Fronkle. 'Don't worry, Loser, I'll take your place!' he burped, and I shrugged his hand off and turned to face the pier, where the captain was waiting.

'All aboard for Mogden Island!' he boomed.

tiny bit wrinkly

Captain Two Fingers

'All aboard for Mogden Island!' boomed the captain again, and I wondered if he just liked saying it, seeing as it was only me and the little girl from my school getting on, and we'd both comperleeterly heard him the first time.

I jumped into his ferry, which was actually just a little wooden boat with a tiny motor hanging off the back of it, and sat down next to the girl. She was looking a teeny weeny bit nervous, and I guessed it must be her first time at Pirate Camp.

bad mood Barry

'It's that boy who was crying!' she giggled up at her mum, who was standing on the pier, but I just ignored them both, because I was too busy looking at the captain's hand.

The captain's hand was at the end of his arm, which is where hands usually are. What wasn't usual about this hand, howeverypoos, was that it only had two fingers.

chopped off

1 2

'See you've seen me fingas!' said the captain, and I immedi-swivelled my eyes a millimetre to the right, so they didn't look like they were looking at his fingers any more. 'Fishies got 'em!' he cackled, nodding out towards the lake, and I wondered if Mogden Lake had sharks in it or something.

'R-r-really?' stuttered the little girl, suddenly not giggling any more, and she stuffed her hands into her pockets for safekeeping.

little girl's pockets

'Nah, jus' pulling ya legs!' chuckled the captain, and the little girl glanced down at her legs, looking like she wished she had somewhere to hide them too.

The captain undid the rope that was keeping the boat tied to Mogden Pier and started fiddling with the motor. He grabbed a handle with his two fingers and gave it a tug, and the ferry started blowing off, little clouds of smoke floating out of its bum.

'Off we go!' he shouted, sticking his hand in the water, right next to the propeller bit, and pulling up the anchor, which is exackerly the sort of thing that gets your fingers chopped off.

'Erm, how long is it to Mogden Island?' asked the little girl, waving goodbye to her mum.

'Two minutes!' said the captain, holding up his two fingers.

Sally Bottom

'Aren't you a bit old to be going to Pirate Camp?' said the little girl, shuffling up to sit next to me.

'My dad thinks I need to grow up,' I grumbled, waving goodbye to Bunky and Nancy and Desmond, but not my dad or Darren.

One of my eyeball gobstoppers dropped out of my pocket and rolled across the ferry floor.

I reached over and grabbed it, plopping it in my mouth, then made an eyehole-shaped hole in the middle of my lips. I twizzled the eyeball round so the little black eye-dot faced the little girl.

← my mouth

'Urgghh! Your mouth's got an eye!' she giggled, and I spat it out and stuffed it back in my pocket.

All of a non-sudden my mum-phone fell out of my other pocket and clunked on to the ferry floor. The little girl looked at it and giggled again.

'What's so funny, little girl?' I said, because I didn't know her name.

'Your phone's pink!' giggled the girl. 'My name's Sally Bottom, by the way. Very nice to meet you!'

imagine this is pink

I picked up my mum-phone, wondering why my pockets were being so useless all of a sudden, and then I realised something. 'Hang on a millikeels, did you just say your name was Sally BOTTOM?' I said, and the little girl nodded. 'But that's like having a BUM for your second name!' I sniggled.

72

The little girl peered back at Mogden Pier, where her mum was still standing, and her bottom lip started to wobble. Then she looked at me the way I look at people when they make fun of MY second name, and I suddenly felt a teeny weeny bit bad.

'Sorry, Sally Bottom,' I said, staring out at Mogden Lake, and I thought how much Bunky would wee his pants when I told him about Sally Bottom's name. Then I clicked my fingers. 'Wait a billisecond, I can call him NOW!' I said, and I pressed the 'redial' button on my phone.

'Darrenofski residence,' crackled Darren's voice after only half a ring.

'Put Bunky on, would you, Dazza,' I said.

'Who's this?' said Darren.

'It's Barry,' I said.

mum phone

Darren phone

'Barry who?' said Darren, like we were doing a knock knock joke.

'Barry Loser,' I said, and Sally Bottom giggled.

'You've got ten seconds, Loserface,' said Darren, and I heard him pass the phone to Bunky.

'Hello?' said Bunky.

'Donald? It's Donald Cox – long time no speak!' I said, and Bunky did a sniggle. 'Donald, you'll never believe what the girl on this ferry is called. Her name's Sally Bottom!' I whispered, so Sally wouldn't hear.

'Sally Bottom? But that's like having a bum for your second name!' giggled Bunky.

playing it keel

'EXACKERLY! So, erm . . . what's going on?'
I said, because I'd already comperleeterly
run out of things to say.

'Not much . . .' said Bunky.

'Go on,' I said, trying to get my ten
seconds' worth out of Darren's phone.

'Well . . . I'm still on Mogden Pier,' mumbled
Bunky. 'I can see you - you're about three
metres away,' he said, and I looked up and
spotted him, Nancy and Darren, standing
exackerly where I'd just left them. My
dad was driving off in his car, and I
imagined him chuckling to Desmond, all
happy that he'd got rid of me.

'What's the weather like over there?' I said, as Captain Two Fingers sped the engine up and the boat started to judder. I did a little leg-waggle dance to stop myself falling over like a comperleet loseroid and spotted Darren, grabbing his phone back off Bunky.

'Bye bye, Bazza,' crackled Darren's horrible little voice, and the phone went dead.

'OK, well, great to catch up, Donald, let's do lunch sometime!' I shouted, pretending to Sally it was me who was ending the phone call, not Darren. Which was perfect timing, because we'd just arrived at Mogden Island.

Morag Barnacle

'Ahoy, me hearties! Let's get ye landlubbers ashore!' roared a voice, and I jumped on to the beach and looked around, trying to spot Burt Barnacle, the unbelievakeely old owner of Pirate Camp.

'Shiver me whatsitcalleds, there's pieces of eight all over the crow's nest!' roared the voice again, except this time I noticed something weird about it. It was higher than Burt's voice, plus Burt never said 'Shiver me WHATSITCALLEDS'. He always said 'Shiver me TIMBERS'.

I **Future-Ratboy**-darted my eyes around the beach and spotted a plastic coconut, sellotaped to the top of a half-deflated blow-up palm tree. 'Burt?' I said, wondering if he'd got so old his head had turned into a coconut.

Burt?

'Down 'ere!' drawled the voice again, and I tilted my head down until I was face to face with a great big fat ugly-looking lady version of Burt, standing underneath the blow-up palm tree.

79

'M-M-Morag!' I stuttered, because I'd only ever seen a great big fat lady version of Burt as ugly-looking as this one once before, and it'd been Burt's unbelievakeely lazy and horrible daughter, Morag Barnacle.

'That's me name, don't wear it out!' chuckled Morag, who looked like she'd squeezed herself into a pirate costume when she was eight years old, then left it on for the next fifty years.

Her arms were covered in tattoos of her favourite junk food, and her fake eyelashes dangled off her eyelids like shrivelled-up tarantulas. Sitting on the end of her hooter was a mosquito, its nose-spike sucking bogie-infested blood out of a hairy nose wart.

hat
stinks

feet
stink

hanky
stinks

'Come on you two 'orrible kids, get
ya stuff off the ferry an' follow me.
You're late already!' she boomed,
turning round, and me and Sally Bottom
grabbed our bags and waved goodbye
to Captain Two Fingers.

81

Nettle forest

'Where's Burt?' I said, trudging after Morag through the forest of nettles behind the beach, towards the campsite. I'd pulled my socks up over my ankles so they wouldn't get stung and was doing my hand-waggle tree impression to stop the mosquitoes from biting me on MY hooter.

'Who's Burt?' asked Sally Bottom, trying to keep up with me on her little legs.

'Burt Barnacle is the owner of Mogden Island,' I said, turning round to Sally. 'He's really nice. He looks like a REAL pirate, with a beard and everything - not like HER,' I whispered, pointing at Morag's big bum.

bum stinks

'Argggh!!!' screamed Sally, scraping her ankle against a nettle leaf, and I remembered MY first time on Mogden Island, before I learned my amazekeel socks-pulling-up trick.

I plucked a ginormous leaf out of the ground and passed it to her. 'Here, put this dock leaf on your ankle - it'll take away the sting,' I said. 'Burt taught me that - it's an ancient pirate trick!'

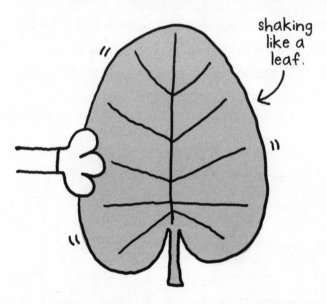

shaking like a leaf.

Sally wrapped the leaf round her leg and pulled her sock up over it. 'Thanks, Barry Loser,' she said, and Morag did a sniggle at my name.

'WHERE'S BURT?' I said again, because Morag had comperleeterly ignored me the first time.

Morag stopped trudging and turned round, sweat waterfalling down her face. 'Me old dad's gone up to the great big pirate ship in the sky, gawd bless 'im,' she warbled, one of her tarantula eyelashes half-hanging off its eyelid.

keel!

I rewound my brain back to when my grandad died a few years before, and remembered my mum saying he'd gone up to the great big SOFA in the sky.

'Oh, Burt,' I whispered, looking up at the sky, trying to spot a pirate-ship-shaped cloud. But they all looked more like sofas.

comfy!

cushion

'What does Morag mean, Barry?' asked Sally Bottom, and I shrugged. 'Dunno,' I said, not wanting to explain it to her, seeing as she was only a little kiddywinkle. And then I realised something.

'Hang on a millikeels,' I said. 'If Burt's floating around up there, who's gonna take over Pirate Camp?'

Morag pointed one of her fat fingers at her face and whipped a smelly-looking hanky out of her pocket.

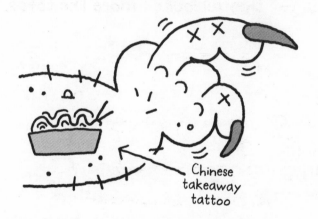

Chinese takeaway tattoo

'Meet the new owner of Mogden Island!' she said, wiping her armpits with the hanky then blowing her nose on it, and I tried to picture her looking after a camp-full of little kids, but couldn't imagine it at all.

'Ere we are

Morag turned back round and carried on trudging, with me and Sally Bottom following behind her, until we got to a clearing. "Ere we are!' she panted, and we stepped out of the trees into a ginormous circle of hardly any trees. I looked around at Pirate Camp, even though I knew what it was like from all the times I'd been there before.

The ground was covered in woodchips, and about eight million kid-sized tents had been put up round the edge of the circle, all facing into the middle.
A rickety old building, exackerly like a pirate ship except more of a hut, sat on the outside of the circle, and I remembered how Burt used to stand on the porch bit of it, making up his ghost stories.

Burt's hut

Sticking out of the hut's roof was a flagpole, and I tilted my head up to look at the skull-and-crossbones flag Burt used to fly off the top of it. 'It's gone all tattered and saggy,' I mumbled, sounding like my mum talking about one of her tops when she's put it in the washing machine on the wrong setting.

view from inside washing machine

Bundled up next to the hut was the parachute we used to sit under while Burt whooshed it up and down. Shiny black slugs slithered over the creases of the parachute, and empty face-painting pots were dotted around on the hut's window ledge, dried-up brushes poking out of them like half-dead blow-up palm trees.

thinks they're
real trees

'Where are all the kiddywinkles?' I said, because I couldn't see any kiddywinkles, which was weird, seeing as this was a kiddywinkles' camp.

'Let's 'ave a look-see, shall we?' said Morag, and she took a big, crackly breath.

91

Loser in the middle

'Yo ho ho! Batten down the thingamajigs, ye bilge-sucking scurvy dogs!' boomed Morag, and twenty-six-and-three-quarter bored-looking kiddywinkles appeared out of the forest and started heading towards us.

'Waaaahhh!!! Twenty-six-and-three-quarter kiddywinkles!' I screamed, mostly because one of them had a quarter of themselves missing. Then I realised it was just a kid wearing a fake wooden stump leg, which had blended in with the trees behind her.

'Arrr! Shiver me whatsitcalleds!' shouted the stumpy-legged kid, who was a scruffy-looking little girl with a patch over one eye. She hobbled up to me and trod on my toe with her stump.

HOBBLE!

'OWWWWAH!' I little-girl-screamed, because it really, really, really, really hurt.

'Ain't you a bit old for Pirate Camp?' said Stump Leg, but I just ignored her and looked at all the other kiddywinkles, wondering who'd been looking after them if Morag had been with us, and Burt was up in the sky.

my view

Morag pointed at a space between a couple of the tents. 'Room for one more over there,' she grunted. "Cept of course there's two of you!' she chuckled, and I wondered where the leftover person's tent would go.

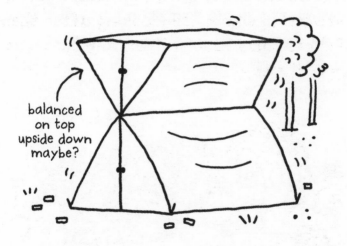

balanced on top upside down maybe?

'Where will the other person's tent go?' asked Sally Bottom, copying what I was thinking, and Morag pointed into the middle of the circle, where all the tents were facing.

'Bagsy not me!' I cried, because who wants their tent to be in the middle of all the other ones, and I zoomed towards the little space, limping because my foot had just been stomped on by Stump Leg.

'Wait for me!' shouted Sally Bottom, speeding past me and diving into the space head first, and I stopped limp-zooming and scratched my bum, wondering what I was going to do now.

ZOOM!

'Looks like it's Loser in the middle!' chuckled a familikeels-sounding voice from behind me.

Gordy-wordy

I twizzled round on my good foot and saw Gordon Smugly - the even-meaner -than-Darren kid from my class at school - appearing from behind a tree.

'Oh, I should've known YOU'D be here, Smugly,' I said, because Morag's all-new Pirate Camp was exackerly the sort of place where someone like him could get away with bossing kiddywinkles around.

Gordon glided over to Morag, acting like he owned the whole island - which he didn't, Morag did.

'Welcome back to Pirate Camp, Loserface,' he said, and Morag patted him on his head.

'Smugly 'ere's me first mate, in't that right, Smugly?' she said, and Gordon nodded.

'Only because he hasn't got any MATES on the mainland,' I said, and Stump Leg did a little snortle.

'Morag is thirsty, Gordy-wordy,' said Morag, lowering herself down on to a log and doing a blowoff at the same time. 'Make a nice mugga tea for 'er, would ya?' she drawled, and I wondered why she was talking about herself as if she was another person.

Gordon clicked his heels together and did a little salute, a bit like the ones me and Bunky do, except nowhere near as keel. 'Coming right up, boss!' he said, tapping one of the kiddywinkles on the head. The kiddywinkle was a boy who was wearing thick round glasses the width of a can of Fronkle.

glasses

Fronkle

'You, boy, come with me!' snapped Gordon, and the kiddywinkle trudged after Gordon, looking like he was enjoying his half term about as much as I was.

100

The missing poles

I limped over to the space in the middle of the circle and dumped my rucksack down on the woodchips. 'Unkeelest half term EVER,' I grumbled, pulling my tent out from the bottom of the bag and emptying all the bits on to the ground.

You know when you're emptying all the bits out of your tent bag and there's that clanging noise from the poles landing on the ground? That wasn't what was happening right now.

'Where's the clanging noise?' I said, looking for my poles. And then I remembered something.

'Oh noooooooo!!!' I cried, rewinding my brain to three Saturdays before, when I'd been using the poles in my garden, pretending to be **Future Ratboy** in the episode where his hometown, Shnozville, is being invaded by really tall, skinny, metal, pole-shaped aliens.

I sat down on a log and put my head in my hands, staring at a woodlouse chewing on a woodchip.

'What's the matter, Barry Loser?' said a little voice, and I looked up to see Sally Bottom wandering towards me with a cuddly Clowny Wowny under her arm. I could see her tent behind her, all put up with its poles included and everything.

wobbliest log ever

balanced on woodchips

'Forgot my stupid poles,' I mumbled.

Sally darted off into the forest and came back three milliseconds later with two pole-length sticks. She stuck them into the ground, fished a bit of string out of my tent bag, tied the string between the two sticks and then draped my orange tent over the top of the whole thing.

kind of keel

'TA-DA!' she said, pressing her cuddly Clowny Wowny's belly, and he did a blowoff.

'Thankskeels, Sally,' I said, stuffing my empty tent bag into my rucksack. A spare bit of string was hanging out of it, and I pulled it out and stuffed it in my pocket, because you never know when you might need a piece of string.

remember for later

Sally looked at me like I'd gone mad. 'What does "thankskeels" mean?' she said, scratching her bum, which is short for 'bottom', which is her second name, and one of my eyeball gobstoppers dropped out of my pocket and rolled along the floor, almost flattening that woodchip-eating woodlouse I was talking about earlier.

SHRIEK!

'It's what **Future Ratboy** says instead of "thanks"!' I said, rummaging around inside my rucksack and pulling out my cuddly **Future Ratboy**, which I'd brought to keep me company once I'd eaten both my gobstoppers.

I pressed **Future Ratboy**'s belly and he shouted 'KEEL!', and Sally stared at him like she'd never seen a cuddly **Future Ratboy** before.

'Please tell me you know who
Future Ratboy is,' I said.

'I know who **Future Ratboy** is,'
said Sally.

'Phew, thank keelness for that!'
I sighed.

Ratboy

Clowny

'I don't really,' said Sally. 'I was just
saying it.'

'OH MY UNKEELNESS!' I cried. 'How
can someone not know who **Future
Ratboy** is?!'

I turned to my cuddly **Future Ratboy** and shook my head. 'Sometimes I wonder what the world is coming to, **Ratboy**,' I sighed, feeling like an old granny. Sally Bottom sat her bum down on my log, which was really only big enough for one loser at a time.

'Don't be sad, Barry Loser,' said Sally, and I looked around at Pirate Camp. Stump Leg was kicking a tree trunk with her non-stump leg, while a couple of other kiddywinkles were throwing stones at an empty, crumpled-up can of Fronkle.

THWUMP
THWUMP

Morag had wobbled off over to her pirate hut and was snoozing in her rocking chair on the porch, getting her toenails cut by a scared-looking kiddywinkle.

'What in the name of unkeelness am I DOING here, Sally Bottom?' I grumbled.

'I thought your dad sent you to grow up?' said Sally, and I laughed, but not the sort of laugh you laugh when you're happy.

'Excusez moi?' said Sally in a French accent all of a sudden, and I twizzled my head round to give her a funny look, then realised it wasn't her who'd said it.

A skinny boy in a stripy jumper with a pointy nose was walking towards us.

us

Renard Dupont

'Bonjour! My name, eet eez Renard Dupont . . .' said the skinny boy in the stripy jumper with the pointy nose, holding his hand out to shake ours.

That makes it sounds like me and Sally had one hand between us. We didn't, we had four.

'Nice to meet you, Renard,' said Sally Bottom, getting up off my log and shaking his hand, and my log did a seesaw, tipping me on to the ground.

FLOOP!

'I'M DOING THIS ON PURPOSE!' I cried, as I landed nose-first in a pile of woodchips, and I immedi-stood up and dusted myself down, not that there was any dust on me, it was mostly woodchips. And a couple of woodlice.

'My name is Sally Bottom,' said Sally
Bottom. 'And this is Barry Loser.'

'My family, we 'ave just moved to,
'ow you say, Mogdon?' said Renard.
'I am sinking maybe I can be making
new friends on zis island?'

'You mean Mogden? That's where we
live too!' said Sally, and I nodded.

'Mogden is the keelest,' I said, acting all
keel because I've lived in Mogden my
whole life and I know absokeely
everything about it.

114

'Zis Pirate Camp - so far eet eez very boring, non?' said Renard, looking around.

I did a little glance around myself and spotted Stump Leg, who'd stopped kicking the tree trunk and was scraping her stump through the woodchips. She was making an 'S' shape, and I wondered if she was spelling out her name, and it actually WAS Stump Leg.

SCRAAAPE!

'BORING, YOU SAY, DO YA?' boomed a voice, and we all looked up at Burt's pirate hut. Morag had shooed away the kiddywinkle who'd been cutting her toenails, and was peering down at us.

'Yeah, boring!' shouted Stump Leg back at her. 'What're we sposed to do 'ere all week?'

bit like a young Morag

'DO WOT YA LIKE, YA LITTLE BARNACLES!' grunted Morag, picking up a holiday magazine and flipping it open. 'TOILET COULD DO WIV A MOPPING,' she snuffled, pointing over her shoulder at a bucket with a smelly-looking mop sticking out of it, and we all looked around at each other, wondering what was going to happen next.

still stinks

117

Toilet mopping

What happened next was that Renard started walking over to the bucket and mop.

'What are you doing, Renard?' I said, because who in the name of unkeelness walks towards a bucket and mop unless they're being forced to?

'Bof, it eez zis or sitting around on our bum-bums doing nothing, non?' he said, picking the mop and bucket up and heading towards the toilet block, which was actukeely more of a telephone-box-sized cupboard over on the other side of the clearing.

quite jealous of hair

'BOF?' I said, wondering what 'bof' meant, since I'd never heard the word before.

'BOF!' said Renard. 'You ask zee silly question, I say "bof",' he smiled, and we all followed him over to the toilet. 'Ooh la la!' he cried, as the door creaked open and eight million mosquitoes flew out, all of them doing blowoffs. Or at least that's what it smelt like.

mosquito
blowoff cloud ➘

'There must be SOMETHING better to do than this,' sighed Sally Bottom, as Renard stuffed the bucket under the taps above the little sink, and I rewound my brain to all the times I'd been at Pirate Camp before.

'When I was a kiddywinkle and Burt Barnacle was in charge, we used to sit around the campfire singing songs about trees,' I said, thinking how keel that'd been - especially compared to mopping a toilet floor.

'Who's Burt Barnacle?' asked Stump Leg, watching as Renard filled the bucket with water and heaved it out from under the taps, dumping it on the ground so that water sploshed all over his trainers. He picked up the mop and swung the wooden pole around, pretending he was dancing with a really skinny old granny wearing a greasy stinking wig, and everybody did a sniggle.

granny mop

'Burt Barnacle is a REAL pirate - with a beard and EVERYTHING!' smiled Sally, saying what I'd said to her in the nettle forest. 'Except he's a cloud now,' she said, pointing up at the sky, and Stump Leg gave her a funny look.

Burt cloud

'Bof! Singing about trees eez for leetle babies, non?' said Renard, dunking the mop into the bucket and slopping it on to the toilet floor, and a woodlouse who'd been gnawing on a toilet roll tube did an eek and scuttled away from the granny's wig.

'That's not all we did!' I said, not wanting Renard to think Burt Barnacle was a loser or anything. 'There was also pirate face-painting and pirate raft-making and lying under Burt's giant skull-and-crossbones parachute while he whooshed it up and down and searching for hidden treasure . . .'

Renard stopped mopping and leaned on the wooden pole. 'Excusez-moi if my leetle ears are playing a treek wiz their owner, but did I just 'ear zee word "TREASURE"?' he said.

'Yeah, except we never FOUND any,' I said, and that was when I sensed something really annoying and smuglyish behind me.

Very bad news indeed

'What's all this unkeelness about?' sneered
Gordon Smugly, appearing from behind
a tree. He was supping on a mug of tea,
trying to look all grown-up, but I could
tell he didn't really like it.

The kiddywinkle with Fronkle-width glasses was standing next to him, holding a tray with sugar sachets, a couple of napkins and those stupid little plastic tea stirrers on it.

no sips taken

'We was just saying how boring Pirate Camp is,' said Stump Leg.

Gordon started to take another sip of his tea, then changed his mind and poured the whole lot on to the woodchips. He went to put the empty mug on the kiddywinkle's tray, then changed his mind AGAIN and placed it on top of his head instead, smiling down all smugly at Sally at the same time.

TRAY-HEAD!

'I don't think we've been introduced?' he said, reaching his hand out to shake hers. 'Gordon Smugly – Chief Operations Manager here at Pirate Camp.'

'Sally Bottom. Nice to meet you!' said Sally Bottom, and Gordon blinked.

'Sally Bottom?' he said, looking like he couldn't believe his luck. 'As in, your second name is Bottom?'

Sally nodded, and her lip started to wobble.

LIP WOBBLE!

'Goodness me! I thought old Barry here had an unlucky name, but BOTTOM - it's like you've got a BUM for your surname!' cackled Gordon, stroking his smug, ugly chin. 'Not only that, but your first name sounds a bit like "smelly", so really, your name is SMELLY BUM!'

A big fat tear rolled down Sally's face.

big
fat
tear

'You can talk, SMUGLY!' I shouted,
saying the 'UGLY' bit of his name extra
loud. 'At least Sally Bottom's got some
friends!' I pointed at Stump Leg and
Renard, and then me.

128

Gordon's eyebrows tilted into their sad positions, but only for a millionth of a billisecond. He ran his hands through his hair and opened his smug, ugly mouth. 'Yes, well . . . you kiddywinkles have your fun while you STILL CAN,' he drawled, doing a weird, non-smiley smile, and he picked his mug up from on top of the kiddywinkle's head.

'What's THAT sposed to mean?' said Stump Leg, and Gordon put his mug back down again.

inside stump

'Oh nothing,' said Gordon. 'Just that Morag is selling Mogden Island to Donald Cox.'

'Donald Cox?' I said, as if I was talking to Bunky. 'Donald Cox, the man who builds buildings all over Mogden?'

Donald Cox, remember?

'Yes, that's right - Donald Cox,' said Gordon.

'What are you talking about, Smugly?' I said, even though it was pret-ty easy to work out what he was saying.

'Let me spell it out for you, Barold,' he sneered, looking down at me like I was a woodlouse. 'Morag Barnacle is selling Mogden Island to Donald Cox, and as soon as Donald Cox gets his hands on it, he's going to turn it into a luxury holiday resort.'

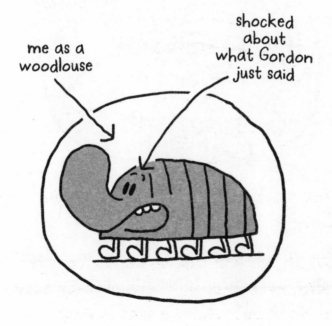

me as a woodlouse

shocked about what Gordon just said

He whipped a shiny-looking, folded-in-three piece of paper out of his back pocket and handed it to me. 'Donald Cox's Luxury Wooden Lodges!' said the words at the top of the little brochure. Underneath was a photo of the clearing where we were standing right now - except instead of tents, there were brand spanking new wooden lodges.

'Pirate Camp is OVER, Loser!' snortled Gordon, and he turned round and slithered off.

Renard's idea

'Wot a loser!' said Stump Leg, then she looked up at me. 'Sorry Barry, not you - I was talking about Gordon Smugly.'

'Don't worry, Stump Leg,' I said, sitting down on a log and glancing over at all the tents. 'No more Pirate Camp - difficult to imagine, isn't it?'

'Eet eez quite easy for me to imagine, Barry,' sighed Renard, dunking the mop back in its bucket. 'Ever since I 'ave been 'ere, I 'ave been sinking . . . what eez zee point of all zees? UNTIL . . .' and then he stopped talking, and we all waited for him to start again.

'Until WHAT?' said Sally Bottom.

'Until I 'eard Barry talking about zee treasure!' smiled Renard.

trees look like mops

'What treasure?' asked the kiddywinkle with Fronkle-width glasses, who was still standing next to us with Gordon's empty mug on his head. He was also still holding the tray with sugar sachets, a couple of napkins and those stupid little plastic tea stirrers on it.

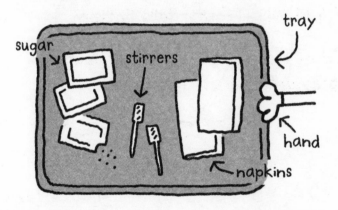

'Barry said he used to go on treasure hunts here when he was little!' said Sally, lifting the mug off the boy's head and putting it on the tray. 'What's your name, by the way?'

'I'm Seymour,' said the boy, and
Stump Leg scrunched her face up.

'Seymour?' she said. 'As in you can
SEE-MORE?'

'If you want,' said Seymour, putting
his tray down on a log.

'Shouldn't you be SEE-LESS?' said
Stump Leg, pointing at Seymour's
Fronkle-width glasses, and everyone
sniggled.

'Well if you're going to be like that about it, I spose my name should be "SEE-THE-SAME-AS-EVERYONE-ELSE-THANKS-TO-MY-GLASSES",' said Seymour, and Stump Leg de-scrunched her face.

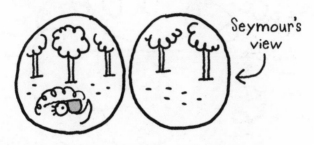

Seymour's view

'You got me there, See-more!' she giggled, and she turned to me. 'So, Barry, wot about this treasure, then?'

'Hang on a millikeels, I didn't say there WAS any treasure - we never FOUND any, remember?' I said, not wanting to get the kiddywinkles too excited. As far as I knew, Burt had made the whole thing up.

'But this is our last chance, Barry!' said Sally. 'Once Donald Cox gets here he'll start digging holes EVERYWHERE to build his luxury wooden lodges. If WE don't find the treasure, he DEFINITELY will!'

getting a bit excited

'Come on, Barry - we'll be rich and famous!' shouted Stump Leg.

'Yeah! Then we can BUY Mogden Island OURSELVES and pay someone NICE to take over from Morag!' said Seymour.

138

'Bof, zee treasure 'unt will be more fun zan mopping, non?' said Renard.

'But I don't know where it is!' I cried.

'You MUST have SOME idea, Barry,' said Sally Bottom, and I stroked my chin.

me stroking my chin

I looked at all the kiddywinkles lined up in front of me and realised something. This was their last chance to have a keel time at Pirate Camp before it was comperleeterly knocked down by Donald Cox.

'Well, I spose I might have a TEENY WEENY one . . .' I said, looking at Burt's rickety old pirate hut.

139

Snoring Morag

'The reason we could never actually FIND any treasure . . .' I said, twizzling my head back round to face the kiddywinkles, 'is that Burt said he could never remember where he'd put the treasure MAP!'

'There's a MAP?' said Seymour, his glasses steaming up with excitement.

'Yep. And if we're gonna find it, our best bet's in there,' I said, pointing at the hut.

hut over there →

Morag was up on the porch, her big fat face snoring underneath her splayed-out holiday magazine. Her newly-cut toenails waggled on the ends of her feet, and a shiver went down my spine. Or maybe it was a leaf sticking out of a tree, scraping against my back.

I peered through the hut's grimy window and spotted a giant set of shelves stacked full of paper. It didn't look like Morag had tidied up AT ALL since she'd taken over from Burt.

'What a dump!' I said, feeling like my dad when he talks about my bedroom. 'No wonder Burt could never find anything . . . but if we could somehow sneak past Morag and have a peek ourselves, maybe we'd have more luck!'

The kiddywinkles' eyebrows all tilted into their scared positions as Renard let go of his mop and it clattered to the ground.

'Let us do zees,' he said.

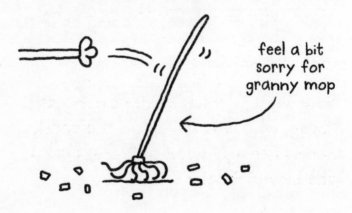

feel a bit sorry for granny mop

Trying to get out of actukeely doing anything

We all tiptoed over to the pirate hut, Stump Leg tip-stumping, but not too loudly thanks to all the woodchips.

'Now what?' I whispered, pointing at Morag, who was still up on the porch snoring her ugly head off, and I did a little blowoff out of fear.

'Zees was your idea, Barry!' whispered Renard, and I shook my head, because it's one thing having an idea and a comperleeterly different thing doing it.

I looked around for Gordon and spotted him on the other side of the clearing, sitting on a log reading a newspaper, pretending to be all grown-up.

actukeely really bored

'Stump Leg, go and distract Gordon!' I said, because the last thing we needed was her stomping around on the porch, waking up Morag. 'Seymour, you and Renard sneak in to the hut and find the treasure map while I stay out here with Sally Bottom and everyone else and keep watch!'

Seymour's glasses de-steamed, and he peered through them at me like I'd gone comperleeterly mad. 'But I'm just a kiddywinkle!' he whisper-cried. 'I can't go!'

nose same size as his head

'Yeah Barry, Seymour's only little!' whispered Sally.

'Alright, alright,' I said. 'I'll go – Renard, are you coming with me?'

'Oui!' grinned Renard, which means 'yes' in French but sounds exackerly like 'wee'.

me thinking he needs a wee or something

Futur garçon de rat

I crept up the wooden stairs to the porch, blowing off with fear on every step, and Sally Bottom giggled, probably because I was reminding her of Clowny Wowny.

'Sank you very much for zat, Barry. NOT!' whispered Renard, who was creeping up the stairs behind me, holding his nose, and I twizzled my head around to look at him.

'You have **Future Ratboy** in FRANCE?!' I said, because he'd just said 'NOT!', and that's what **Future Ratboy**'s sidekick, Not Bird, says.

'Ooh la la, but of course!' said Renard. 'In my country, 'e eez called "**Futur Garçon de Rat**",' he grinned, doing his best **Futur Garçon de Rat** face, and I had to hold in a sniggle as I tiptoed past Morag.

Futur
Garçon
de Rat

I pushed against the wooden door and it creaked, and Morag snuffled underneath her holiday magazine. The photo on the front of it was of a beach a bit like Mogden Island's, except this one looked much hotter, like it might have real coconut trees instead of fake blow-up plastic ones.

'Morag eez planning une vacation, non?' whispered Renard, nodding at the magazine, and I imagined her jetting off on holiday with her suitcase full of Donald Cox's money.

'Not if we can help it!' I said, stepping into the hut.

The broken mirror

'Ooh la la, mon unkeelness . . .' whispered Renard, looking around inside the hut and doing a little whistle. 'Zere eez a lot of, 'ow you say . . . junk, non?'

I Future-Ratboy-unzoomed my eyes out so I could take it all in. 'Sure iskeels,' I said, wondering if Burt had been like one of those people on TV who can't throw anything away.

I tiptoed round a pile of empty yogurt pots, over to the shelf stacked full of paper I'd spotted through the grimy window. The corner of a yellowy treasure-map-lookingy sheet was sticking out of the pile, and I imagined myself as a magician whose main trick was being able to find treasure maps really easily.

just thinking how keel I am

'Abracadabra!' I whisper-shouted, closing my eyes and pulling out the yellowy sheet. I held it up in the air and opened my eyes, getting ready to see the treasure map, but it was just a boring old gas bill.

'Eet will not be zat easy, Barry,' smiled Renard, walking over to a fridge and opening the door. 'Sometimes, zee sing you are looking for, eet eez een zee place you least expect.' He poked his head in and looked under a packet of mouldy sliced cheese.

I rolled my gobstopper eyeballs in my pocket, then my real-life ones to myself in a little mirror on the wall. The mirror was cracked, which didn't surprise me, seeing as Morag probably looked in it every morning when she was sticking on her tarantula eyelashes.

'Eet looks as eef somebody 'as 'ad zee bad luck, non?' said Renard, pointing at the crack, and I nodded, because everyone knows breaking a mirror is bad luck.

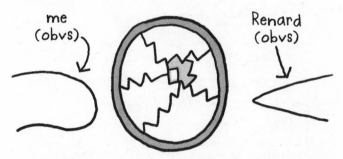

me (obvs)

Renard (obvs)

'Burt, I spose . . .' I whispered, then I did a freeze-frame, like when you pause **Future Ratboy** on TV.

Peeking out of a gap in the cracked mirror, just above where my freeze-framed nose was being reflected, was a tiny triangle of yellowy paper.

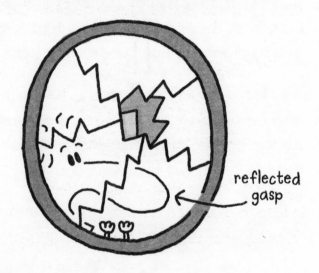

reflected gasp

'Renard, do you see what I see?' I said, tiptoeing over to the mirror.

"Ow could I see what you see, Barry?' said Renard. 'You 'ave your eyes . . . and I 'ave mine.'

I lifted the mirror off the wall, and immedikeely realised it was about seventeen times heavier than it looked. The frame slipped through my fingers and crashed on to the wooden floor.

'Zat eez even worse luck, non?!' whisper-shouted Renard, and I heard Morag snuffling around on the porch.

'Woss all the racket?' I heard her grunt, as I looked down at the broken bits of mirror scattered around my feet. I could see my face, reflected a million times, peering back up at me. And lying in the middle of all the pieces was a yellowy-looking map.

Abraca-dabkeels

'It's Burt's treasure map!' I cried, picking it up and stuffing it in my pocket. 'He must've hidden it here, then forgotten all about it!' I laughed, and then I stopped laughing, because I remembered that Morag had woken up.

"Oo's in there?' boomed Morag, and I heard her great big fat feet stomping towards the wooden door.

'Run for eet, Barry - I will deal wiz Morag!' Renard shouted, and I tilted my nose forwards into its extra-fast position.

'Abracadabkeels!' I cried, as the hut door flung open.

'You wait till I get me 'ands on you!' cackled Morag, standing in the doorway like a ginormous podgy door with its legs wide open, and I dived between them out on to the porch.

podgy
Morag
door

157

Run for it

I ran down the wooden steps and looked around for all the kiddywinkles. 'Psst! Barry!' whispered Sally, and I spotted them all, hiding behind a particukeely wide tree trunk.

'Where's Renard?' asked Seymour as I crouched behind the tree next to them, and I pointed at the hut, just as the grimy window opened.

Renard's head poked out, then his arms, then the whole rest of his body.

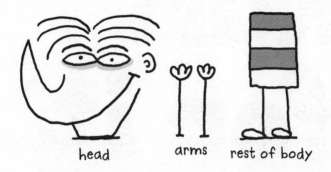

head   arms   rest of body

'Zis Morag, she eez une crazy lady!' he cried, as he fell on to the porch and Futur-Garçon-de-Rat-forward-rolled down the steps over to us.

Morag squidged herself back out of the door on to the porch and looked around. 'Gordy-Wordy, where are ya, boy?' she hollered, and I spotted Gordon on the Nettle Forest side of the clearing, looking at Stump Leg, who was distracting him by waggling her hands in the air, pretending to be a tree.

'What is it, boss?' warbled Gordon, putting down his newspaper and standing up.

'WOT IS IT?' grunted Morag. 'THOSE BLINKING KIDDYWINKLES BEEN RUMMAGING ROUND IN MORAG'S PERSONAL BELONGING-FINGS, THAT'S WOT. NOW GO GET 'EM, BOY!' she roared, stomping her foot down on the porch, and it crashed straight through the floorboard.

CRUNCH!

'Run for it!' cried Stump Leg, hobbling away into the forest of trees, and I zoomed after her, everyone else behind me.

160

Loser Island

'I think we've lost Smugly for now!' I shouted, as we all skidded to a stop next to a ginormous dead tree, its crooked branches reaching into the sky like ancient granny arms. I pulled Burt Barnacle's map out of my pocket and held it up for everyone to see.

'You found it!' gasped Stump Leg, then she started chuckling.

'What's so funny, Stump Leg?' I said, because this really wasn't the time for chuckling - Gordon was running after us, and we needed to find the treasure before Morag sold Mogden Island to Donald Cox.

'Mogden Island - it looks just like you, Barry!' laughed Stump Leg, and I flipped the map round to face my face.

'GAAAH!!!' I screamed, because Stump Leg was right - Mogden Island was EXACKERLY the same shape as my head.

Renard peered over my shoulder. 'Stomp Leg, she eez correct, non?' he said, pointing at the bit of the map that showed the forest of nettles.

'Zees is your 'air,' he muttered, ruffling my hair. 'And zees is your face, Barry,' he smiled, waggling his finger over the middle of the island, where all the tents were.

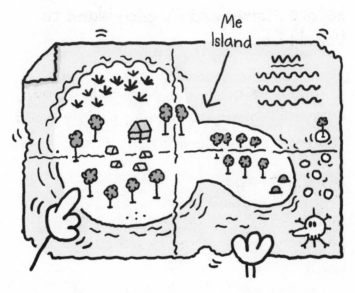

Me Island

'And ZEES . . .' he carried on, moving his finger over to a huge bulge of land that I didn't even know existed, 'zees is your big nose!'

The kiddywinkles all snortled, and I
tried to shrink my nose a centimetre,
which I don't know if you've ever tried
to do it, but it isn't easy.

'CURSE THE SHAPE OF MOGDEN ISLAND!'
I cried, waggling my fists up at the sky
like the dead tree's branches, and I
Future-Ratboy-darted my eyes around
on the map, looking for a cross.

'Where's the X?' I said, because
treasure maps always have an X on
them somewhere - to tell you where
the treasure is.

'Zere eez no X, Barry,' muttered
Renard, stroking his chin. 'Only zees
leetle scribbles . . .' he said, pointing at
the top right hand corner of the map.

The clues

I peered at the top right hand corner of the map. There, written in tiny, wobbly little capitals, was the word 'CLUES', with three sentences underneath:

CLUES

Follow ye nose with the tips of ye toze.

When ye are there, ye should have a good stair.

Pick ye bogie care-fully. The wrong one and you'll get smel-ly.

'I can seeee yooou!' cried a familikeels voice from behind us, and I **Future-Ratboy**-unzoomed my eyes out from the clues and poked my head up from the map.

'It's Chief Operation Manager Smugly!' screamed Sally Bottom, as Gordon appeared from behind a tree.

'What's that smelly bit of old paper, Loser?' sneered Gordon, and I **Future-Ratboy**-speed-folded the map in half and stuffed it in my pocket, hoping he'd forget he'd ever seen it.

'It's a TREASURE map!' said Seymour, his glasses steaming up again.

'Treasure, eh?' said Gordon, still panting from running after us. 'Well, if there's any treasure on THIS island, I think it should go to Chief Operations Manager Smugly!'

'Treasure THIS!' shouted Stump Leg, stomping on Gordon's foot, and he crumpled on to the ground like a smug, ugly deckchair. 'RUN FER IT!' she cried, hobbling off in the direction of the island's nose.

Which seemed like a good idea to me, so we all followed her.

Bogie Islands

I whipped the map back out of my pocket and started re-reading the first clue, which isn't an easy thing to do when you're running behind a load of kiddywinkles.

'Stupid wobbly writing!' I shouted, shaking my fist as we all skidded to our stops on the edge of a beach.

'This isn't the beach we landed on with Captain Two Fingers,' said Sally, looking around.

'Where ARE we, then?' cried Seymour.

I looked down at the map and tried reading the first clue again. '"Follow ye nose with the tips of ye toze . . ."' I muttered, 'But what in the name of unkeelness is a "toze"?'

Stump Leg looked at me like I'd gone mad.

'It's the first clue!' I said, and I looked back up at the beach. Sticking out of the sand were two giant rocks, covered in seaweed.

'Hey! They're the nostrils on Mogden Island's nose!' I grinned, pointing at the nostrils on the map, then at the rocks.

'"Follow ye nose with the tips of ye TOES..."' said Sally Bottom. 'Isn't that what we just did?'

I looked at Sally, trying to work out what she meant. 'What do you mean, Sally Bottom?' I said, and she giggled.

'We just used the tips of our toes to get to the island's nose!' she said, and I rolled my gobstopper eyes, because 'toes' had been spelled 'toze' on the map.

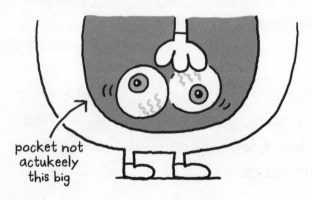

pocket not actukeely this big

'What kind of loseroid wrote these clues?' I groaned, then I realised it was probably Burt, so I did a quick back-to-front-salute at a passing cloud, just in case it was his pirate sofa ship and he was watching.

just a totally normal cloud

'WHAT NOW?' cried Seymour, as I peered down at the wobbly writing on the map and read out clue number two.

'"When ye are there, ye should have a good stair . . ."' I said, and I scratched my head, looking around the beach for some stairs.

'Stare - zees eez when zee person eez staring out to sea, non?' said Renard, staring out at the lake.

stare line

'No, Renard, that's spelt S-T-A-R-E,' I said, carrying on looking for some stairs, but I couldn't see any. The only interestikeels-looking things were the nine or ten tiny little mini islands sticking out of Mogden Lake, a couple of metres off the tip of Mogden Island's nose. They were mostly made out of rock and had slimy green seaweed growing all over them.

172

those islands I was just talking about

'Hey, those little islands look like bogies!' giggled Sally Bottom, pointing at them on the treasure map.

'Eeew,' said Seymour, pushing his glasses up his nose, and I giggled, realising something.

'Hang on a millikeels, it was stupid old Burt and his spelling again - he meant "STARE", not "STAIR"!' I cried, staring out at the bogie islands, and Renard tutted.

'Zis eez what I am saying all along, non?' he sighed.

'These are the worst clues EVER, Barry Loser!' said Stump Leg, doing a little mini-stomp on my foot, and I was just about to do a mini-scream when I spotted clue number three out of the corner of my eye.

'I've got it! It's the bogie islands! The treasure must be on one of the bogie islands!' I shouted.

shell, not poo

Smelly bogies

'Huh?' said Sally Bottom, scratching her bum. 'I don't get it, Barry Loser.'

'Look!' I said, pointing at clue number three. '"Pick ye bogie care-fully. The wrong one and you'll get smel-ly." We have to pick a bogie island – and the least smelly one, by the sound of it!'

I started wading out into Mogden Lake, then stopped, sensing something annoying behind me. 'Gordon!' I gasped, looking over my shoulder, because Gordon Smugly was up at the top of the beach, panting.

'The treasure will be MINE!' he shouted, flinging his hands out wide like Donald Cox, and he started hobbling towards us all slowly, limping from his stomped-on foot.

Gordon
Cox

'NEVERRR!!!' I shouted in my keelest pirate voice, stepping forwards with my right foot, and the whole leg that was attached to it disappeared into the lake.

SPLOSH!

'WAAAHHH!!! BE CAREFUL OF THE FISHIES, BARRY!' cried Sally Bottom, stuffing her hands into her pockets for safekeeping, and I remembered Captain Two Fingers telling us how he lost his fingers.

'Don't worry Sally, Captain Two Fingers was only joking!' I shouted over my shoulder, and I felt something nibbling at my leg.

'WAAAHHH!!! SHARK!!!' I screamed, then I realised it was just my mum-phone, vibrating in my pocket. I whipped the phone out, breathing a sigh of relief that it'd been in my left pocket which was still dry, and I pressed the 'answer' button.

about to press answer button

'Donald Cox!' crackled Bunky's voice.

Bunky, remember?

'Donald Cox!' I sniggled, even though there wasn't really time for any sniggling.

'Donald, just checking in – long time no see!' said Bunky, and I looked back at the others. Renard, Stump Leg, Sally Bottom, Seymour and all the other kiddywinkles were right behind me, with Gordon just behind them.

I pulled out the piece of string I'd stuffed in my pocket earlier that day and threw it over to Renard. I pointed to some logs that'd rolled down the beach out of the forest. 'Tie those logs together with this string to make a pirate raft,' I cried. 'Load the kiddywinkles on to it and follow me!'

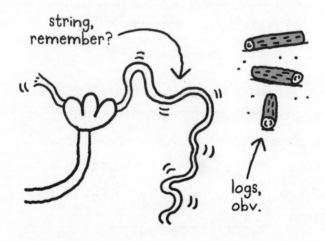

string, remember?

logs, obv.

'Oui oui, Captain Barry!' grinned Renard.

'Stump Leg, see what you can do about Smugly!' I shouted, and Stump Leg immedikeely whipped off her wooden leg and started using it to scoop a ginormous hole in the beach's sand.

leg all relieved to be out

'What's all this unkeelness?' said Gordon, hobbling up to the edge of it, and Seymour gave him a push from behind. 'WAAAHHH!!!' screamed Gordon, falling ugly-face-first into Stump Leg's pit.

I gave Stump Leg and Seymour a quadruple-salute and turned back to my phone.

'Donald, I'm a little tied up right now,'
I said to Bunky, swimming over to the
first of the bogie islands and having a
sniff around. Which isn't as easy as it
sounds, seeing as I was using one of my
hands to hold my mum-phone out of
the water. 'I'm looking for a
non-smelly bogie island, Donald,'
I said, as if that was a comperleeterly
normal sentence.

crocodile
style

'Not a problem, Donald,' said Bunky.
'Just wanted to fill you in on the Poo
Tour - we're having a fantastikeels
time over here!' he crackled.

'That's great, Donald!' I said, except it came out as 'Dat's date, Donald!' because I was holding my nose, what with the stink of the seaweed growing all over the first bogie island.

hair looks kind of keel

'Nancy's dad knows EVERYTHING about flowers and insects and stuff, Donald!' warbled Bunky down the phone, and I nodded, pretending I was listening. 'It's not all about poo - that's just a way to get people like me and you interested.'

I held the phone away from my ear
and gave it my bored-face look, the
way I do when my granny calls me up
to talk about her day.

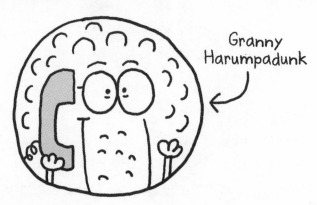

Granny
Harumpadunk

'Anyway, Donald, let's hook up for
lunch sometime soon!' I said, wondering
if Bunky had turned into a comperleet
loseroid without me there to keep him
keel, and I hung up.

'This bogie island stinks!' I shouted over
my shoulder to Renard and the others,
and I started swimming towards the
next one.

Everyone dig!

'This one's no good either - it's comperleeterly covered in seaweed!' I shouted, as I got to the next bogie island. Except I didn't say it as clearly as that, because I'd put my mum-phone in my mouth to carry it.

Renard had tied four logs together into a pirate raft and was paddling it towards me, with him, Sally Bottom, Stump Leg, Seymour and all the other kiddywinkles wobbling around on top of it.

'What about the one over there?' cried Seymour, nodding at a slightly bigger island about three and three quarter metres away. It was made out of sand instead of rock, with nothing growing on it apart from a single tree sticking out of the middle.

like a cloud on a stick

'It won't stink – it's the only one without any seaweed on it!' shouted Sally.

'Eet eez our only chance, Barry!' panted Renard, paddling towards it, and I twizzled round in the water. I started swimming over to the sand island, spotting Gordon, who'd climbed out of Stump Leg's hole by now and was super-smugly-speed-swimming behind us.

really slow

The raft bumped into the sand island at the exact millisecond I got to it too, and we all clambered on to the sand, me waggling my nose around in the air to make sure it didn't stink.

'Not smelly at all!' I said.

'Quick everyone, dig!' shouted Stump Leg, whipping off her wooden leg and starting to scoop, and the rest of us started digging holes in the sand with our hands, like we were on the shortest summer holiday ever and wanted to make the most of it before going home.

'Nothing!' I panted, sticking my nose into my treasure-less hole, which was exackerly as deep as my nose, which is pret-ty deep.

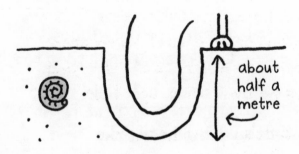

about half a metre

'Me neither!' groaned Sally Bottom.

'We must not geeve up!' cried Renard, who was standing in his hole, his head sticking out the top of it, and I spotted Gordon, wading out of the water on to the sand island.

Gordon
Soggly

'Stand back, you little losers, Gordy-Wordy is here!' he sneered, dropping to his knees and starting to dig his own smug, ugly hole.

And that's when I heard the scraping noise.

Smallest treasure chest ever

'TREASURE!' shouted Stump Leg, and we all twizzled our heads round, apart from the ones who were already facing her. 'It's a treasure chest!' she beamed.

I jumped into Stump Leg's hole, followed by Sally Bottom, then Seymour, then Renard. She'd dug a pret-ty big hole, in case you hadn't realised.

'Quickly!' giggled Sally, scraping sand away from a dome-shaped wooden lid at the bottom of the hole, and we all joined in until we'd uncovered the smallest treasure chest any of us had ever seen. I don't know why it needed four of us to scrape the sand away, actukeely.

like a massive pocket

'MINE! THE TREASURE IS ALL MINE!' warbled Gordon, trying to squidge himself into the hole with us all, but luckeely there wasn't any more room.

'There'll never be enough treasure in there to make us rich!' groaned Seymour, as Stump Leg lifted the chest out of the hole. Sally Bottom's bottom lip started to wobble.

'You must be positeeve, Zeymour!' cried Renard, as Stump Leg lifted the lid and everybody gasped.

even
treasure
chest
gasping

Biggest letdown ever

You know gasps? Sometimes they aren't because something's amazing.

'Ooh la la, zees is a big letdown, non?' said Renard, as we peered into the chest.

It wasn't like the treasure chest was empty or anything. It was comperleeterly full.

It was what it was full of that was the problem.

'WOODCHIPS?!' I cried. 'Who in the name of Mogden Island needs more WOODCHIPS?!'

The storm

A humungaloid cloud, kind of the same shape as a pirate ship, floated over, and little raindrops started to pitter-patter on to the surface of the lake.

'NOW what?' said Sally, as we all floated back to Mogden Island on the pirate raft, Stump Leg holding her treasure chest full of woodchips.

Gordon waded out of Mogden Lake and limped up on to the beach after us, looking a teeny weeny bit embarrassed about how excited he'd been about the treasure. 'I TOLD you lot there wasn't any treasure!' he shouted, and we ALL rolled our eyes.

'Spose we just sit the rain out in our tents?' I said, holding out my hand. A raindrop landed on it and I slurped it up, seeing as I hadn't had a sip of water all day.

SLURP!

196

We trudged back into the forest, no-one really saying anything much at all, and I kicked a twig, feeling all let down about the treasure. 'Looks like we won't be buying Mogden Island after all. Sorry if I got your hopes up, kiddywinkles,' I said, my nose doing a droop.

'It's not your fault, Barry Loser,' said Sally Bottom, giving me a smile, then all of a sudden the smile turned into a lip-wobble, and she started patting her pockets. 'Clowny Wowny!' she wailed. 'Where's my Clowny Wowny gone?'

lip wobble times a millikeels

A raindrop splatted on to Seymour's glasses and he wiped it away with his sleeve.

SPLAT!

'Last time I saw him, we were hiding from Morag behind that extra-wide tree. Maybe you dropped him there?' he shrugged, which seemed like a good idea to me, so we all headed back to it, seeing as there wasn't anything else to do.

Furry hand

We skidded to our stops next to the particukeely wide tree. Not that we really skidded, because you can't skid when all you've been doing is trudging.

'All kiddywinkles successfully captured and returned to camp, Captain Morag!' smiled Gordon, running in front of us and doing his rubbish salute, and I rolled my soggy gobstoppers, because it hadn't been him who'd brought us back, we'd come back on our own.

'Good work, Gordy-Wordy,' grunted Morag, who was still sitting on her porch, reading her holiday magazine. 'I'll deal with you 'orrible lot later,' she breathed, peering down at us through her tarantulas. 'In the meantimes, Donald Cox'll be 'ere soon. Give the old camp a sweep for me, wouldya?' she said, pointing at a stack of brooms.

'Sweep THIS, fat bum!' shouted Stump Leg, turning her treasure chest upside down, and the woodchips tumbled out on to the ground.

Morag got up off her rocking chair, then sat back down again.
'Suit yerself . . . 's'not like it's gonna make any difference once Donald Cox starts knocking the 'ole place down!' she cackled.

stinks

I looked around at Pirate Camp and sighed. A raindrop sploshed on to the end of my nose, and I wondered if maybe it was one of Burt Barnacle's tears. After all, this place had been his pride and joy.

'Clowny Wowny, where are you?' cried a little voice, and I snapped out of my daydream and spotted Sally Bottom scrabbling around in the bushes.

I Future-Ratboy-zoomed my eyes around, looking for her cuddly toy, and I was just about to give up looking, mostly because looking for cuddly toys is comperleeterly boring, when I spotted something familikeels and furry-looking, sticking out from under a bush.

'Clowny Wowny?' I said, tugging on Clowny Wowny's hand, and I pulled Clowny Wowny out.

'Sally, I've found Clowny Wowny!' I said, holding Clowny Wowny up above my head.

feel like a kiddywinkle

And that's when I saw the thing that was about to make me scream.

Giant wood-louse

'WAAAHHH!!! GIANT WOODLOUSE!!!' I screamed, dropping Clowny Wowny and doing my world-famous leg-waggle dance.

I was doing my leg-waggle dance because, scuttling out from under the bush towards Stump Leg's woodchips, was the ginormerest woodlouse I'd ever seen.

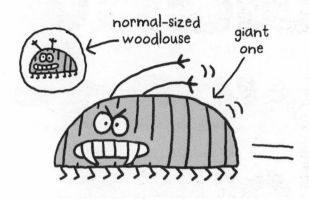

normal-sized woodlouse

giant one

'Clowny Wowny!' beamed Sally, jumping over the giant woodlouse, and she ran up to me. She picked Clowny Wowny off the ground and gave him a cuddle, and I wondered if I could sneak off to my tent and give my cuddly **Future Ratboy** a quick hug, because the giant woodlouse really had given me a shockypoos.

'Thank you, Barry Loser!' said Sally, and I shrugged.

'It was nothing,' I said, pretending I hadn't just screamed and done my leg-waggle dance like a comperleet loser.

'And thank you for making Pirate Camp so fun today,' said Sally, and Stump Leg, Renard and Seymour all nodded.

'Yeah, Barry, that was the best time ever!' said Seymour. 'I wish YOU were in charge of Pirate Camp!' he smiled, then he glared at Morag, not that she was taking any notice.

206

'Thankskeels, kiddywinkles!' I smiled, my nose undrooping, and I gave myself a mini-upside-down-salute in my pocket.

'Unfortukeely, I don't think I'll be able to take over Pirate Camp though,' I said, and just as I was wondering when Donald Cox was going to turn up and take over Mogden Island, one more raindrop hit me on the head and made a lightbulb turn on inside my brain.

CLICK!

my giant brain

Brilliant and amazekeel idea

'Wait a millikeels,' I said, pointing at the giant woodlouse, and everyone stopped talking, not that they'd been talking that much anyway.

'What eez eet, Barry?' asked Renard, walking over and putting his head next to mine, trying to see what I was seeing.

'The giant woodlouse!' I cried, pulling my mum-phone out of my pocket.

Renard scratched his head and looked at me. 'Bof. I am not understanding zees, Barry . . .' he said, but there wasn't time to explain.

long arm much?

I **Future-Ratboy**-speed-dialled Darren's number and the phone rang three times, then did a click. 'This is Darren Darrenofski, I'm busy playing it keel right now, please leave a message,' said Darren's voice, then there was a beep.

'Darren, this is Barry, I need to talk to Bunky!' I cried, and I hung up. I slotted the mum-phone back into my pocket and it started ringing. 'That was quick,' I muttered, pulling it back out and pressing the 'answer' button.

'Donald Cox?' I said.

'Donald!' sniggled Bunky, and I did a sniggle back, even though there wasn't time for sniggling.

really happy
to be chatting
to each other

'Donald, listen up,' I said. 'Donald Cox is taking over Mogden Island. I need you to get over here - right now!'

'Donald Cox?' said Bunky, not sure if I was talking to him, or about the real-life Donald Cox.

'That's right - Donald Cox, Donald Cox!' I said, beginning to confuse myself. 'Look, there isn't time to explain. Just get on the ferry - and bring Nancy and her dad with you too!'

me
hanging
up →

SLAM!

Real-life Donald Cox

I slotted the mum-phone back into my pocket. The rain had stopped pitter-pattering and the sun appeared from behind a sofa-shaped cloud.

'What's the big idea, Bazza?' said Stump Leg, and then she gasped.

I twizzled my head round and did another one of those gasps you do when something bad has just happened.

Standing in front of me was the real-life Donald Cox. He was carrying a briefcase and wearing one of those hard yellow hats people wear when they're about to knock down a Pirate Camp.

'It's Donald Cox!' cried Seymour, and Donald Cox held his arms out wide.

what's in here?

'Somebody say my name?' he boomed, taking off his sunglasses and grinning, his bright white teeth flashing like a shark's. His eyes were smaller than I'd expected, and much closer together.

taken hat off too

'Had a shocker getting through those nettles, Morag!' he chuckled, and I glanced down and spotted two dock leaves tucked into his socks.

'Welcome to Pirate Camp!' shouted Stump Leg, running up to him and stomping on his toe.

'Arrrggghhh!!! Nobody treads on Donald Cox's toes!' screamed Donald Cox, even though Stump Leg just had.

Gordon glided over from the pirate hut with three mugs of tea on a tray - one for Morag, one for Donald Cox, and one for himself.

only non-chipped one for Donald

'Sorry 'bout our little friends, Donald,' drawled Morag, handing Donald Cox a mug and taking one herself. 'Soon as we sign the papers I'll be calling their mums and dads to pick 'em up!' she chuckled, and I looked at the time on my mum-phone.

'Come on, Bunky!' I whispered to myself, and I peered into Nettle Forest, waiting for his nose to come bobbing through the trees.

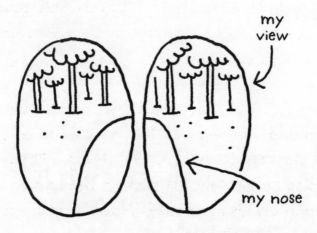

my view

my nose

Fake
fingernails

I carried on peering into Nettle
Forest for another ten minutes –
enough time for Donald Cox and
Morag to finish their mugs of tea, and
for Gordon to pour his away when he
thought no one was watching.

'So . . . that's the chit-chat done!' said
Donald, looking at Morag's tattoo of
a chicken drumstick and doing a little
face to himself. He clicked the locks
open on his briefcase. 'Now to get
down to business!'

He opened the briefcase lid, and everybody gasped. Again.

The whole inside of it was filled up with money - not the shiny gold coins you get in treasure chests though. This was paper money, enough to buy the whole of Mogden Island in one go.

'Oooh, that is luvverly, Donald!' grunted Morag, stroking the notes with her fat hand, and one of her raggedy old fake fingernails fell off, lying there on top of them like a bright red shiny dead woodlouse.

'Urrgghhh,' shivered Donald Cox, turning his small, close-together eyes away from the nail. 'Anywaaay . . . shall we get this over and done with, Morag?'

'Get WHAT over and done with?' asked a familikeels voice, and I looked up and saw Bunky's face.

'Bunky!' I cried, calling him 'Bunky' instead of 'Donald Cox' for the first time in about two weeks.

'Barry!' grinned Bunky. He was standing next to Darren, who was standing next to Nancy, who was standing next to her dad, Mr Verkenwerken, who was standing next to the particukeely wide tree trunk, looking like he was wondering what he was doing there.

Donald Cox closed the lid of his briefcase and Morag yelped. 'What's all this craziness about?' he said, looking at Bunky, Darren, Nancy and her dad.

Morag heaved herself up off the log she was squatting on and took a puff on her asthma pump. "Oo are you lot?' she breathed, and Bunky, Darren, Nancy and Mr Verkenwerken all looked at each other, then at me.

ERM...

Mr Verkenwerken, nature expert

'Let me explain what's going on here,'
I said, crossing my fingers and hoping
my brilliant and amazekeel idea was as
brilliant and amazekeel as I thought it
was.

I walked over to Mr Verkenwerken
and gave him a wink, and he peered
down at me and wrinkled his forehead,
the way dads do when they're trying
to remember if they've met one of
their kids' friends before.

'Mr Verkenwerken here is Mogden's number one expert on nature,' I said, pointing at his outfit, which was green shorts with loads of pockets in them, a pair of really long pulled-up white socks, a green short-sleeved shirt with even more pockets than the shorts, some binoculars round his neck, and a magnifying glass that was hanging from his belt.

(go back 2 pages)

Everybody nodded, and Mr Verkenwerken stood up straight and put his hands into two of his pockets, looking all pleased with himself.

'I haven't got time for this, little boy!' boomed Donald Cox, pulling a pen out of his inside pocket. 'Let's sign these papers, Morag – I've got a meeting in thirty on the other side of Mogden.'

He clicked the end of his pen and pulled a folded-up piece of paper out of his jacket pocket. He handed the pen to Morag and grinned his bright white teeth.

'Good finking, Donald,' snuffled Morag, scribbling her name on the dotted line. Donald snatched the pen back and held it a millimetre above the page.

'Er, you might want to think about that, Donald,' I said, as he moved it a billimetre closer to the paper.

1 billimetre

'Donald Cox doesn't think!' said Donald Cox. 'Donald Cox DOES!' and he was just about to sign his name when I whipped Gordon's little luxury lodges brochure out of his smug, ugly back pocket.

Donald Cox's Luxury Wooden Lodges

'Ah, I see you've seen my brochure!' laughed Donald, his hand doing a freeze-frame, and I held the brochure up for everyone to see.

'Bunky, would you be so kind as to read out what it says on the front cover?' I said, and Bunky Future-Ratboy-zoomed his eyes in on the brochure.

'Donald Cox's Luxury Wooden Lodges!' said Bunky, looking all proud of himself, even though all he'd done was read out some words.

'Thank you, Bunky,' I said, folding the brochure back up and tucking it into MY back pocket, just to annoy Gordon.

Donald Cox waggled his eyebrows and held his arms out. 'And your point is, little boy?' he asked, peering down at me.

waggle city

I stroked my chin, pretending to think a bit, even though I knew exackerly what I was going to say.

'Now, there's one word on that brochure of yours that interests me, Donald,' I said, whipping it out of my pocket again. I don't know why I put it away really, seeing as I was going to get it out again so quickly.

'And which word is that?' said Donald, looking at his watch. Morag was standing behind him, her arms folded, looking all annoyed at me.

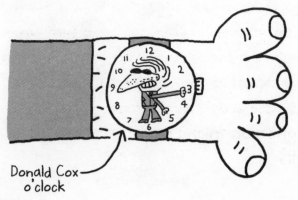

Donald Cox o'clock

'WOODEN!' I boomed, slapping the brochure against the particukeely wide tree trunk, and Mr Verkenwerken blinked.

'Wooden? Yes, they'll be wooden lodges - the finest in Mogden!' said Donald Cox, getting ready to start signing again.

'Which brings me to Mr Verkenwerken here,' I said, pointing at Nancy's dad.

'Me?' warbled Nancy's dad, looking nervous. 'What've I got to do with this?'

'Nothing to worry about, Mr Verkenwerken,' I said, patting him on the arm and leading him over to Stump Leg's woodchips, where the giant woodlouse was still chomping. 'I just thought you might be interested in THIS . . .'

Giant Sabre-toothed Woodlouse

You know how there are good gasps and bad gasps? Well I'm not sure which sort of gasp Mr Verkenwerken did when he saw the giant woodlouse, but it was a BIG one.

'GIANT SABRE-TOOTHED WOODLOUSE!' cried Mr Verkenwerken, pointing at the woodlouse. 'IT'S A GIANT SABRE-TOOTHED WOODLOUSE!' he shouted, and Donald Cox clicked his pen shut.

'Say that again?' said Donald Cox, even though he'd comperleeterly heard it the first time - plus Mr Verkenwerken had shouted it again after that.

'It's a Giant Sabre-toothed Woodlouse!' beamed Mr Verkenwerken. 'They're extremely rare!'

all proud of itself

'I KNEW your dad'd know what it was called!' I said to Nancy, giving myself a quadruple-reverse-salute.

Bunky wrinkled his forehead up,
looking like he didn't understand.
'I don't get it!' he said, and all the
kiddywinkles nodded.

'Well,' I smiled, starting to explain my
brilliant and amazekeel idea. 'You know
how this woodlouse has been eating all
the woodchips?' I said, and Bunky
blinked. 'And you know how Donald
Cox's wooden lodges are gonna be
made out of WOOD?'

thick as a
plank of
wood

'Ye-ah . . . ?' said Bunky, and I rolled my gobstoppers, because he STILL didn't get it.

'Well, WHO would want to build a load of luxury wooden lodges on an island that's covered in GIANT-LUXURY-WOODEN-LODGE-EATING WOODLICE?' I cried, and everyone went quiet.

my big moment

Nose droop

For about seventeen and three quarter milliseconds, the only noise on Mogden Island was the chomping of woodchips coming out of the Giant Sabre-toothed Woodlouse's mouth. And then Donald Cox started to clap.

'Verrrry clever, little boy,' he said, smiling to himself, and I wondered why he was smiling when I'd just comperleeterly ruined his dream of an island full of luxury wooden lodges.

'Why are you smiling, Donald Cox?' said Sally Bottom, copying what I was thinking, and Donald Cox stopped clapping.

'I'm afraid your pal's little idea has one BIG problem,' he grinned, looking over at Nancy's dad. 'Mr Verkenwerken, do you want to tell the kiddywinkles or shall I?'

Mr Verkenwerken looked at me all sadly and scratched his bum.

SCRITCH
SCRATCH

'These giant woodlice things eat WOOD, right?' I said, and Nancy's dad sighed.

'They DOOO . . .' he said, '. . . but Giant Sabre-toothed Woodlice only eat ROTTEN wood, Barry.'

totes rotten

Donald Cox whipped the brochure out of my hand and held it up. 'Donald Cox did his research, little boy . . . and there's not going to be ANYTHING rotten about his Luxury Wooden Lodges!' he beamed. And I felt my nose droop so much it was almost touching the ground.

236

Darren's phone

'That's that then!' beamed Morag, unfolding her arms and coming back to life like a robot whose rusty old batteries had just been replaced.

Donald Cox clicked his pen and hovered it above the dotted line, just below Morag's scribbly signature. 'All we need now is an autograph from yours truly and we've got a deal!' he said, sneering at me.

'Not so fast, Mr Cox,' said Nancy's voice all of a sudden, and Donald Cox froze.

'Wot's up NOW, fer cryin' out loud?' warbled Morag, who'd pulled her hanky out and was giving her armpits another wipe.

Nancy had sneaked Darren's phone out of his pocket and was staring at its screen. 'Oh nothing, I've just been looking up a few facts about the Giant Sabre-toothed Woodlouse,' she smiled, handing the phone over to her dad, and his eyebrows shot up his forehead.

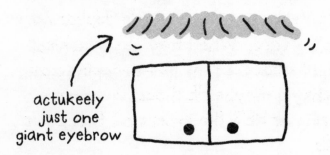

actukeely just one giant eyebrow

238

'Oi, that's MY phone!' snarfled Darren, but Nancy's dad just ignored him and carried on staring at the screen.

'WHAT'S it say, Mr Verkenwerken?' asked Sally Bottom.

good question

'Apparently the Giant Sabre-toothed Woodlouse is a protected species,' said Mr Verkenwerken, a smile appearing on his face. 'Who knew!' he chuckled, and I scratched my still-drooping nose, thinking maybe HE should've known, seeing as HE'S the expert on things like this.

239

'Ooh la la, un protected speesheez!' whistled Renard. 'What does zees mean, Monsieur Verkeenwerkeen?'

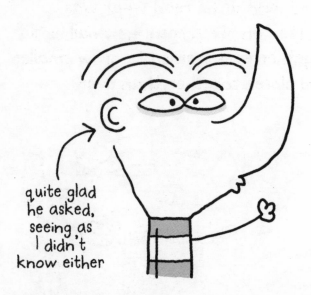

quite glad he asked, seeing as I didn't know either

'It means Mr Cox here won't be able to build his luxury wooden lodges after all,' said Nancy's dad. 'Mogden Island's pristine environment must stay exactly as it is, so as not to interfere with the Giant Sabre-toothed Woodlouse's natural habitat,' he grinned.

240

'What? Let Donald Cox have a look at that!' said Donald Cox, snatching the phone out of Mr Verkenwerken's hand, and as he read what was written on the screen, his small close-together eyes seemed to grow smaller and closer together than ever.

shaking like a leaf, even though it's a phone

'Donald Cox will NOT forget this!' he boomed, whipping his sunglasses out of his jacket pocket and sliding them back over his eyes.

He ripped his piece of paper up into
a trillion pieces and threw them on
the ground next to the Giant Sabre-
toothed Woodlouse, which immedikeely
turned round from its pile of woodchips
and started chomping on THEM instead.

thought it
only ate
rotten
wood?

'Looks like we found some treasure
after all!' grinned Stump Leg, pointing
at the woodlouse, and my nose
de-drooped.

'GAAAHHH!!!' screamed Donald Cox, throwing Darren's phone on the ground and slamming his briefcase shut, and he marched across the clearing, towards the forest of nettles.

hat back on

'Bye bye, Donny-Wonny!' I sniggled, as he disappeared behind a tree.

Loser Camp

"Ere, Donald! Please come back, Mr Cox!' grunted Morag, wobbling after Donald Cox, then giving up and plonking her big fat bum down on a log.

I turned to the kiddywinkles and grinned, the way **Future Ratboy** does when he's just got rid of a really bad baddy.

'Three cheers for Barry Loser!' giggled Seymour, and I did my world famous leg-waggle dance, which is a bit like gasping, seeing as you can do it for good things as well as bad.

the leg-waggle dance™

Sally Bottom wandered over, smiling up at me. 'You make me laugh, Barry Loser!' she said, and I patted her on the head for being such a good kiddywinkle.

'Bunky, Nancy, this is Sally Bottom,'
I said.

'So YOU'RE the famous Sally Bottom!
Keel name!' smiled Bunky, and Sally
gave him a back-to-front-reverse-
upside-down-salute.

I introduced everyone else to
Bunky and Nancy, apart from the
kiddywinkles whose names I didn't
know, and then we all comperleeterly
ran out of things to say.

246

'So what's gonna happen to Loser Camp NOW, eh Loser?' snuffled Darren, cracking open a can of Cherry Fronkle, and I glanced over at Morag, feeling sorry for all the kiddywinkles because she was STILL in charge of Pirate Camp.

my view

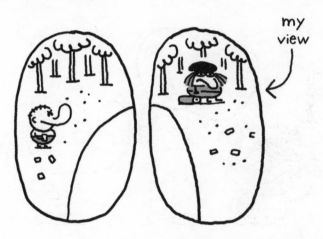

'Who knows,' I grumbled. 'It's not like I can be here every half term. If ONLY there was somebody NICE who would buy Mogden Island off of Morag . . .'

'Hmmm ... funny you should mention that, Barry,' said Mr Verkenwerken, and he smiled the way someone smiles when they've got something keel to say. 'It just so happens that my nature club, The Mogden Association of Plant, Insect and Animal Poo Enthusiasts, is looking for new headquarters ...'

getting
an idea

He looked over at Burt's old hut and stroked his chin. 'I reckon with a lick of paint that old place might do the trick - as long as Morag's up for it, of course!'

Morag grunted and shifted her bum on the log. 'I'm sure we can come to some kind of money-terry arrangement,' she said, peering over at her magazine, and I imagined her going off on holiday, except with The Mogden Association of Plant, Insect and Animal Poo Enthusiasts' money stuffed inside her suitcase instead of Donald Cox's.

Morag in the back, weighing it down

'Er, Mr Verkenwerken?' I said, wobbling on to my tiptoes to look as grown-up as possible. 'This nature club headquarters - do you reckon it'd maybe have space for a teeny weeny little Pirate Camp smack bang in the middle of it?'

'I don't see why not!' grinned Nancy's dad. 'In fact, I've always quite fancied myself as a pirate . . . you wouldn't by any chance be needing a new leader, would you?' he asked, and I imagined Burt up on his cloud, giving him a thumbs up.

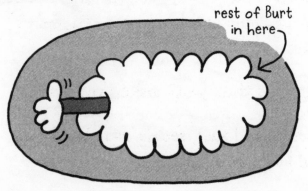

rest of Burt in here

'Maybe Pirate Camp isn't so bad after all,' said Bunky, looking around. 'As long as there's no songs about trees!' he laughed, and I was just about to give him a high five when my mum-phone started to ring.

RIIINNNGGG!!!

I pulled it out of my pocket and pressed the 'answer' button. 'Loser residence?' I said.

'Barry, is that you?' asked my dad.

'Speaking,' I said, seeing as it WAS me, and I was speaking.

'Just checking in - how's it all going?' he said, and I explained everything that'd happened, leaving out the bit where I did my scared leg-waggle dance.

'Sounds like you've really grown up, Barry!' chuckled my dad. 'Which is perfect timing, because your mum's back tomorrow! Great Aunt Mildred's nose has shrunk back to normal, so if you fancied coming home . . .'

my dad

all tired from looking after Desmond

I looked over at Bunky and Nancy and
Renard and Seymour and Sally Bottom
and Stump Leg, but not Darren.

Mr Verkenwerken was on the phone
to Mrs Verkenwerken, telling her he'd
be staying on Mogden Island for a few
nights, just to get the hang of things.
And Morag and Gordon had already
started packing.

'Erm . . . I think I might just stay here a couple more days,' I said, and I was just about to stuff the phone back into my pocket when I remembered something. 'Oh, but Dad?' I said.

'Yes, Barry?' said my dad.

'Tell Desmond his big brother'll be home soon!'

thumbs ups

THE END.

For Pirate Camp.

Until next half term.

About the author and drawer

Jim Smith is the keelest kids' book author and drawer in the whole world amen.

He graduated from art school with first class honours (the best you can get) and went on to create the branding for a sweet little chain of coffee shops.

He also designs cards and gifts under the name Waldo Pancake.

Jim has also got three legs.

Not really, he just needed something to fill this bit with.

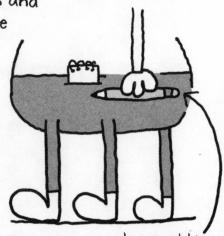

always got his pencil and pad